ALL THAT GLITTERS ISN'T GOD

THE GIRL WHO DIDN'T KNOW IT WAS GOD CALLING HER

IYWANA WRIGHT

DIVINE Flow PUBLISHING

www.IywanaWright.com

First Edition Paperback December 2020

Divine Flow Publishing Ltd, 71-75 Shelton Street,

Covent Garden, London, WC2H 9JQ United Kingdom

www.DivineFlowPublishing.com

ISBN: 978-1-9162513-5-9 Paperback

Dedicated to the children of
Esther Children's Home, Ghana.

Dedicated to the women who; prayed, fought, stood still to see the salvation of The Lord and carved out a well-trodden path, now arrayed with beautiful flowers, rich anointing and powerful stories as an example for Women in Ministry to follow.

INSPIRATION

This book was inspired by our relationship with God and by the Women in Ministry who share their stories, testimonies and journey in Ministry in Ordained Magazine. This is the story we wish we had heard when we were younger.

CONTENTS

Chapter 1 9
The Worst Summer Holiday Ever
Chapter 2 11
Saying Goodbye to Mum and Dad
Chapter 3 17
The Tall Gold House
Chapter 4 23
A Pinteresting Quote
Chapter 5 25
First Impressions
Chapter 6 31
Did He Just Say...
Chapter 7 33
First Sam Chapter WHAT?
Chapter 8 39
Anyone for Green Banana Bread
Chapter 9 43
Pouty Fish Lips
Chapter 10 47
A Conversation with God
Chapter 11 53
The Unintentional Detective
Chapter 12 57
In the Garden Room
Chapter 13 61
Puzzle Pieces
Chapter 14 65
It's the Police!
Chapter 15 71
Eliza the Aunt's Need for speed
Chapter 16 77
The Livestream Sam Wished was a Dream
Chapter 17 85
God of the Impossible

Chapter 18 93
The Salvation Prayer
Chapter 19 101
Samantha's Dream
Chapter 20 105
Women Should Be Seen and Not Heard
Chapter 21 111
The Call

Notes 117
About the Authors 119
Also by the Authors 121
Glossary 123
Discussion Questions 127
Question 1 129
Question 2 131
Question 3 133
Question 4 135
Question 5 137
Question 6 139
Question 7 141
Spiritual Gifts 143
The Voice of God 145
Becoming a Christian 147
Salvation Prayer 149
Prophets in the Bible 151
A Charity Close to our Hearts 153

CHAPTER 1

THE WORST SUMMER HOLIDAY EVER

"Come on Aunt Eliza, please, wake up!"

We rushed through the streets in the ambulance, sirens blaring, at what felt like 100mph.

The voices around me just felt muffled. I couldn't comprehend anything.

This beautiful lady, my precious godmother, laying right in front of me on her stretcher!

We're slowing down, where are we? The hospital...

* * *

What started out as the best six-week summer holiday ever, turned into the worst!

I turn eleven in two days, I'm about to start high school, now I'm battered and bruised, everything has changed. This is the absolute worst.

I'm still shaking. The last thing I remember screaming was, "WAIT, AUNT ELIZA, LOOK OUT!!!" Now we're here, everything is a haze, ouch, I feel sore all over.

The ambulance doors fly open and they're wheeling Aunt Eliza out, wait, is she ok? Her eyes weren't open. Is this even real? It feels like a bad dream. This whole holiday feels like a bad dream!!

* * *

Let me take you back to the beginning, to where the story really begins. Six weeks ago.

CHAPTER 2

SAYING GOODBYE TO MUM AND DAD

WEEK ONE

"SAMANTHA Get a move on!" Mum shouts from downstairs. She only calls me that when she's getting annoyed with me. Usually she calls me Sam or baby girl.

6:01am

The house is buzzing with movement, activity and excitement this morning. It feels like everyone is on fast forward and I'm in slow motion. What? Brush my teeth? Eat breakfast? I just feel numb.

I have been bouncing off the walls with excitement for weeks, but it literally hit me like a tonne of bricks this morning. I've changed my mind; I don't want them to go and I don't even want to go to Aunt Eliza's anymore. I just want everything to stay the same!!

Aunt Eliza is my godmother, I think she's Mum's second cousin or something. Mum always says I look just like her, I think that's because we have the same big, thick, black, curly hair. Every time I think about her, I have a warm, calm feeling. Somehow, she's no non-sense yet softly spoken.

She's not very tall but people say she's a Power-House in the spirit. She keeps teasing me not to get any taller, "you'll be as tall as me the next time I see you," she says every time she sees me. Mum spent a lot of time with her and her twins last year when her husband passed away. More for emotional support than anything else. I overheard Mum saying, because they sold their successful business a few years before, "they are well taken care of!" Every time she says it, she has a big smile and her eyebrows raised high to Dad, I think that means they have a lot of money.

6:19am

Sounds like Aunt Eliza has arrived, I can see suitcases making their way into the back of her large seven-seater car.

Oh, yeah, my case, wasn't I supposed to…

. . .

6:20am

"Samantha, come on baby girl, you really need to speed things up, your breakfast is getting cold and I told you to bring your bags down over an hour ago. Come on, pick up the pace, we're leaving in 10 minutes!! Don't forget your phone charger and PLEASE put your toothbrush in your wash bag!" Mum said all of that as she spun around my room like a whirlwind, doing ten different things all at the same time and then she was off with my bags down the stairs. Wait, what did she tell me to do?

6:21am

Suddenly, at my bedroom door stood Aunt Eliza, my beautiful godmother. I love her so much, she always looks so classy and elegant from head to toe, like she's on her way to Harrods for Afternoon Tea. Her toe nails are pretty pink, matching her manicured finger nails. The pink compliments her beautiful brown skin perfectly. Today she's actually dressed down; wearing jeans, an oversized white shirt, a simple, gorgeous, long, gold necklace with a single gold leaf hanging down. I know that's real gold!

Aunt Eliza has driven all the way from Kensington in London to my house in Milton Keynes (an hour North of London) ,to come and collect us. Then, she will drive us an hour to Heathrow airport, and finally, the two of us will go back to her house; my home for the next six weeks. I'm pretty sure we could fly from England to New York and back in that time. What a long day this is about to be.

. . .

I was snapped out of slow-motion mode and ran to give her the biggest hug. I don't know what it was, her presence, her warm smile or suddenly no longer feeling alone. Mum and Dad were leaving but this was the one person that was staying. She smelt like flowers and felt like home. I'm no longer trying to balance on water by myself, Aunt Eliza is here. She's my solid ground. Everything is going to be okay.

6:23am

Even in the midst of the hustle and bustle of the house, she took some time out for me, sat on my bed and asked me about the posters on the wall. We had a chat for what felt like an hour, but it was probably only two minutes, but it's the two minutes I needed this morning.

6:30am

We're in the car. "Breathe Samantha," I whispered to myself. Dad says a prayer and it reminds me of the bigger mission. God's presence always makes me feel so calm. Gosh, I didn't even pray this morning:

"Dear God, thank you for this mission, thank you for Esther Children's Home and all the children's lives that will be so much better because of Mum and Dad's work. Thank you for Aunt Eliza. Please be with me and let me have the best time. Let me not be scared, help me to be brave and to remember that with you I am never alone. In Jesus name, Amen".

. . .

I smiled and my eye caught the back of a shiny magazine in the back-seat pocket, an advert I think; ***"always with you!"*** Hmmm.

7:48am

FINALLY, we've arrived. That felt like the longest car journey to the airport. I knew the dreaded goodbye was coming. Maybe I'll just stay in the car and let Aunt Eliza go with them into the airport – no – but then, I'll just be sitting here in the car alone. I'll go into the airport, I love airports, but I hate goodbyes, oh this is so hard!

I may not always show it in the best way, but I love my parents. Dad is an Assistant Pastor and he writes books and articles. Mum is an entrepreneur, which basically means she runs her own business, which is a construction company; they build homes and offices. Mum's latest project, she calls her, 'pet project', it's a massive home and school in Ghana called; "Esther Children's Home". They're going over to meet the builders, start work on the foundation and spend time with the children, it's so exciting. One day I will go and meet all the children we have been praying for.

8:10am

I thought there would be lots of queuing at the airport and that it would be really busy. This is not what I imagined at all.

There were no queues! It was super quick! One conversation at one desk, now we're at Departures!! They're saying goodbye to me, what is happening? I'm numb again. Everything is in slow motion or is it me? I'm waving at my parents. I can't breathe, I want to cry.

8:25am

"They'll be back soon," Aunt Eliza reassured me. I turned to her stunned, again, her words shook me back into reality. I willed myself not to blink. If I blink, I will cry a river. "Come on Sam!" I told myself, "you're nearly eleven years old, keep it together!"

CHAPTER 3

THE TALL GOLD HOUSE

Aunt Eliza would always send me birthday and Christmas cards with £10 or £20 inside.

I've heard Aunt Eliza has a big beautiful house in Kensington, London, there are four floors. I giggled to myself, and thought, it should have a lift like my old Barbie Dream House. I went there when I was about five years old, but I don't really remember it.

I was quiet for most of the journey (apart from my unnecessarily long tutorial to Aunt Eliza on why she should turn off the passenger airbag before she allowed me to sit in the front seat of her car). I wanted to talk more, I had so many questions, but didn't know what to say. Plus, I was sad to be away from Mum and Dad. This is the longest I've been away from them, but I'm also happy that they have this amazing opportunity to do what they love.

Aunt Eliza asked me the best question, and then I couldn't stop talking. The question: "If you could do anything for your birthday, what would it be?"

I started talking about how excited I was that Mum and Dad would be back two days before my birthday. On the actual day, Mum said I could open my presents first, she would then make my favourite breakfast. We are going to see The Lion King in London and then have a meal at a restaurant with my two best friends, I can't wait.

"We're nearly there," Aunt Eliza interrupted me mid flow.

The houses were beautiful and colourful. It was like driving through a rainbow; some pink, some pastel blue and so tall, I hadn't noticed in between all my chatting. Colourful plant pots hang from some of the window boxes. The streets were really clean, it looked like one of those pretty houses in Mums' magazines. There were steps leading up to front doors over basements which looked like whole houses within themselves.

. . .

On my street, every house is the same. It's nice but you could fit my house into Aunt Eliza's about four times.

We slowed down, which colour of the rainbow would we stop at? Pale blue, yellow, pink, green? We're here, Aunt Eliza's house is yellow! The way the sun hits it, it looks gold! It's glowing!

We parked up right outside this beautiful tall, gold house.

"Here we are pumpkin, your home for the next six weeks". We unloaded my cases and walked up the stairs leading to the front door, it felt like a stairway to Heaven.

Aunt Eliza unlocked, then swung the door open! I know I'm just in the hallway, but I am IN LOVE WITH THIS HOUSE ALREADY!!!!!

We arrived at the house later than planned due to a massive accident on the motorway, so Aunt Eliza is rushing explaining she needs to get dinner started before the twins get home from their friend's house. "They're due back any minute now," she sang lining up my last bag and closing the front door.

. . .

Aunt Eliza has twins, they're older than me, a boy and a girl, Harry and Patricia. They're 15, I haven't seen them for a long time, but I've seen pictures. I'm excited to meet them and super nervous, all at the same time.

Copying Aunt Eliza, I slip off my sandals and line them up next to hers. I then try to keep up as we have a whistle stop tour of the house. The decor is stunning, everything is so coordinated and clean. Cream, white and beige, with a themed colour in each room. I'm trying to take it all in slowly, while running to keep up; the front room is huge, the back room too. Wow - there's a chandelier over the dining room table and now we're in this massive kitchen! I'm picturing the food and laughter we'll share this summer. Ok I might get lost in this house!!

"Grab a bag, let's head upstairs," Aunt Eliza instructs, as I act like I can keep up with her energy and speed.

The stairs are steep, and the cream carpet is so bouncy, there must be springs under each step. I take a look up the stairs, then lean into the banister looking up as far as I can see. It looks like so many stairs; this house must lead up to Heaven. Who needs to go to the mountain top to pray when you can just climb to the top of Aunt Eliza's house and meet God there, I laughed to myself.

. . .

We're upstairs and there's another lounge, ok that's sitting room number three. Aww, and an office. I relax, but Aunt Eliza then heads up another flight of stairs explaining things as she goes. I'm not taking it in anymore, this is information overload and I'm trying to act like I'm not tired from lugging these bags up two flights of stairs.

"Here's my room. Harry's is there and Patricia's is that one," Aunt Eliza points out. It's amazing how much I can tell about them from their rooms. Ok, if I'm honest, I want to go jump inside Aunt Eliza's bed. I've never seen such a fluffy, puffy duvet. I'm pretty sure wrapping up in that duvet will feel like being wrapped up in the arms of God. It literally looks peaceful in that room. WOW!

Harry and Patricia are twins, but their styles are very different. His room has a super chilled vibe, I like it. White and clean, furniture in all shades of grey and blue, not fussy, oh and a cool neon sign that says, "Chill," makes sense!! Patricia's on the other hand, is probably the wildest room in the house; there's such a vibrant, fiery energy compared to the rest of the house. Strong, bold, clashing colours, posters with words, there is so much going on. It's a sensory overload but I'm trying to wrap my head around it because I want to get it and I want to like it, I do, I think. I hope she likes me. I hope she doesn't think I'm boring!

. . .

Ouch, I just felt the, 'I-miss-Mum-and-Dad' pang in the pit of my stomach. I haven't thought about them since I arrived. Is that bad? Or does it show that I'm comfortable and happy? Am I? I think so. They must be flying now.

"Please keep them safe Lord. Let them have an amazing time and come back safely home to me, in Jesus name, Amen".

Dad said every time I think about them; say a prayer, if I feel worried, lonely or afraid; say a prayer, if I'm happy or excited; say a prayer, lol. When the Bible says pray without ceasing, he really takes it literally. It's better than worrying all day, I guess. Thanks Dad, it worked, I feel better.

CHAPTER 4

A PINTERESTING QUOTE

"And this is my prayer room, but it's all yours while you're with us," Aunt Eliza offers. "Get comfortable, and make it your own. In fact," she continued, "I have an empty picture frame that needs filling. Maybe you could find and print something on that interest-pin-thing". "You mean Pinterest Aunty!" I corrected, and we both burst out laughing as she headed to the kitchen to get dinner started.

WOW, I have my own room here!!

I'm humming away to myself, unpacking my clothes and quickly filling up my reserved drawer spaces and loading hangers with clothes while imagining all the fun we'll have this summer. Almost finished and I take a break to sit on my new, comfy, luxurious bed to have a flick through Pinterest (or as Aunt Eliza calls it "interest-pin" lol).

As soon as I open the Pinterest App and searched for 'Quotes' immediately, a gorgeous quote jumped off my phone screen and virtually landed in my room! My heart burst, this is it, (or is it, because that was too fast), yeah it is, this is the one! I saved and printed it off via bluetooth immediately. Went to the office down the hall and and there it was, I grabbed it off the printer. Gosh this feels so efficient. Back in MY room - that sounds so good - I figured out how to open the back of the empty picture frame, inserted my quote and hung it in the space directly opposite my bed. Took three steps back... IT'S PERFECT!

The quote is gold and glittery and it reads:

"All that glitters isn't gold". To be honest, I wasn't paying much attention to the words, mainly the gorgeous glitter. Oh yeah, I just remembered the house is yellow too, oh I mean GOLD.

The twins will love this quote as much as me, or not, maybe they'll love it, maybe they won't even notice, we'll see.

CHAPTER 5

FIRST IMPRESSIONS

What's that? The front door, voices, excitement. My heart is racing. Will they like me? What will I say? It's going to be amazing; I hope.

Shall I stay here or go downstairs, I'll stay, no I'll go, I'll go.

Ok, slowly down the staircase. The voices get louder and clearer. I can see feet, legs and hear the excitement. I've heard them ask a few times, "is she here?"

Oh no, they've spotted me.

. . .

"Hi Samantha," Patricia sings. "Hey," Harry said shyly. I smile and raise a few of my fingers to give a tiny wave. My voice is shaky, but I manage to whisper, "hi".

Patricia runs up five steps to meet me with the biggest hug. WOW she likes me. "SHOES!" Aunt Eliza warns. "Sorry Mum," Patricia says tip toeing back down the last few steps, acting like she's not touching the plush carpet with her outdoor shoes. She turns to me and rolls her eyes, and we have a giggle.

"Go wash your hands for dinner," Aunt Eliza smiled at us, looking really pleased we were already getting along. With a spring in her step, she disappeared off again down the hall to the kitchen, singing a song I didn't recognise. Instantly, the twins silently mimic her; song, face and action perfectly!! Oh my gosh, it's moments like these, even though they're not identical, they are undeniably twins. We burst out into silent laughter. I'm in! We're already having private jokes and banter. Fears are easing and I'm relaxing, my guard is dropping. This really is going to be the best summer ever.

Look at me, all independent and grown up! Yep, this time last year I was getting ready to be double figures, now, I'm on the countdown to my 11th birthday. Six weeks and counting. Birthday, then new high school a few days after, so much change. It feels like I'm going to be a whole different person!

. . .

Harry and Patricia are so bubbly and excited. Patricia is taller than Harry and looks a good two years old than him, she looks like a model! Her hair is golden brown with loose curls that hang down her back. She is beautiful, I'd love to have even half of her confidence. Now Harry on the other hand, has piercing brown eyes, the deepest dimples, freckles all over his face and moments of being super quiet and intense, Patricia's opposite. They are much lighter than Aunt Eliza. They have their Dad's rich, ivory beige skin tone and Harry has his dark, wavy hair.

We figure out our seating for dinner, help to set the table and bring in our plates. It smells wonderful. I could stay here forever. Ok, let me not get carried away in this moment and forget my lovely home, Mum, Dad and my friends. But this feels so lovely and special.

It's great to hear about Harry and Patricia's day. They ask me about Mum and Dad. Picturing them as I talk, and remembering them makes me feel even more at home, like they are part of this adventure. They ask me about my house and Patricia turns to her Mum, "can we go visit soon?" "Sure, definitely before the end of the year," Aunt Eliza replies, "I've already said to Sam's Mum we need to do better at making time to visit each other".

WOW, my mind went into overdrive, and in seconds I planned out their entire trip to my house; where they would sleep, meeting my friends, going to the cinema. My youth group would LOVE THEM! Oh, I can't wait for them to come. I know I just got here, but I want them to come to my house right now lol. We have so many exciting adventures ahead of us, I can feel it.

After our minted lamb dinner, we make ice creams with all the toppings. The twins show me their rooms. Again, how different they are is so apparent. Harry showed me his guitar but is too shy to play, "it was my Dad's…" I sensed his sadness. I just stood there for a few seconds, but it felt like an eternity of silence which was broken by Patricia plunging her strong arm through mine, spinning me around and skipping me up the hallway to her room, or shall I say, her world.

She bounced from one side of her room to the next, reeling off story after story about friends, boys and flicking through her phone to find additional references to add context to her stories and put faces to names. I could not keep up, so I just chose to stay in the moment, that way, my face didn't look like I was trying to remember everything, like I was revising for an exam.

Patricia's room without Patricia was hard to understand, but once she was in there, WOW, everything came together and made sense. I could tell how much she loved her room, her space, her stuff and especially HER PHONE. I think we took about 20 selfies together that night. It was fun. I hope she doesn't post me on social media, my Dad keeps saying he doesn't want me on there and that I'm too young. It should be fine, I'm sure she would ask my permission before posting on there, right?

CHAPTER 6

DID HE JUST SAY...

It's been a whirlwind of a day. Patricia talked me through how to use the shower and where to find fresh towels.

Finally, bedtime, I'm shattered. What a LONG DAY!! I thought I'd want to stay up past 10pm, but it's 9:48pm and I'm done!

I knocked on Aunt Eliza's bedroom door. "Come Pumpkin". How did she know it was me? She sat up in bed and paused her audiobook. She has hundreds of books in the office. She said she loves reading but finds Audiobooks easier these days, interesting.

I said good night to Aunt Eliza, and she tapped the bed for me to sit and she prayed with me. "I know the first night in a new place is always the hardest Pumpkin, but you will be just fine".

I headed to my room, my phone was on my bed, it flashed and then stopped. That's weird. I checked it. DAD!!! I gasped, and as I went to unlock my phone and call back it rang again; I nearly dropped the phone in my excitement. Slow down Sam, calm down I said to myself, press the green button.

"DADDY!" I wanted to cry. I know I usually call him Dad, but this was a Daddy moment. "We've arrived baby girl. Well, we've just landed but I wanted to call you as soon as we were allowed to turn on our phones. I know you're probably heading to bed soon". I smiled so I could fight back the tears. "Ok Daddy," I replied, wanting to tell him everything but in the moment able to say nothing. "I have to run, get some sleep baby girl, and tell me about everything in the morning," Dad said.

I feel like he totally understood. "Love you baby girlll!" Mum shouted quietly in the background. "Love you too Mum!" I responded, then went on, "it's been great Dad, I met the twins, the house is massive and…" I suddenly found my words, but Dad had to go. "Tomorrow, tomorrow, tell me all about it tomorrow and remember ***all that glitters isn't gold***. Get some sleep, it's been a long day. Love you, bye". He hung up.

What… did… he… just… say!

CHAPTER 7

FIRST SAM CHAPTER WHAT?

WEEK TWO

Church was amazing. Aunt Eliza said the building had been newly decorated for about a month. It was bright and colourful with purple carpet and cream walls with pretty, (or Mum would say elegant) pictures with scriptures on it.

I was so busy looking at the images on the wall that I nearly walked into this large wooden sculpture of the globe, unhelpfully positioned - I thought - near the doors to the church. "Careful," said Patricia, putting her hand on my shoulder. "You're supposed to walk around the world, not end up in it... get it!" She laughed; a little bit harder than I thought was necessary.

. . .

Sunday School was fun. ***We learned God speaks to us through words, circumstances and when we pray.*** The Youth Pastor said our homework this week was to write down what we wanted to say to God, then ask God to speak to us when we read our Bible and pray. He explained, we may feel a verse of the Bible is an answer to prayer, or some words or a picture may come to mind. We should write it down and ask God what it means and who it's for.

I didn't know I could talk to God that way or that there were so many ways He could talk to me.

I walked out of the class in a bit of a daydream, when I heard, "Hey Sam". I turned around and saw Harry jogging towards me. He'd been in the older Youth class with Patricia. He had offered to sit in class with me, but I declined. People always assume because I'm an only child I get lonely, but actually, I quite like my own company.

"How was Sunday School?" Harry enquired. "Yeah good, we learnt about hearing the voice of God," I replied. "Really! I don't remember being taught that in your class!" Harry looked genuinely interested and as if he was about to ask something, when Patricia came bouncing across with such force, she nearly pushed Harry over, which would have sent me flying!

. . .

"Philippians 4:1 Stand firm in the Lord, beloved," she jested, pretending to march on the spot like a soldier. "Well, you'll never be a soldier in God's army if that little tap can send you flying," Patricia said, throwing shade Harry's way.

"That wasn't funny Patricia!" Harry scolded, as he looked to see if I was okay. "And you're a fine one to talk," he continued, "always good at quoting scriptures, but you might as well be quoting Shakespeare for all the difference it makes!" Harry said rather boldly. "Alright chill out, no need to be sensitive," Patricia replied. "Don't call me sensitive!" Harry shouted! Patricia held up her hands as a sign of surrender. "I was only messing with ya!"

She looked at me and gave me a half smile. "How's it going Sam? You enjoying yourself?" In my excitement I started to explain, "yeah, I was telling Harry…" Patricia interrupted, "Sam, I was only being polite, I'm not really interested". "Oh", I said, feeling a bit dejected. "Don't get me wrong," she said emphasising her words with her hands. "I'm sure it was fascinating, but you know when you've heard it a million times," she said rolling her eyes. "Come on" Harry said leading the way, "let's go inside for the main service before Mum wonders where we are".

* * *

When the twins weren't trying to distract me by pulling silly faces behind Aunt Eliza's back, I was able to take in the service and realised I had never felt the presence of God like this before. It was hard to describe, it felt light and calming, but also happy and safe, all at the same time.

Then the Pastor started to speak about the Bible. "Please turn your Bibles to First Sam..."

I thought I'd be bored; this part of the service usually feels more like it's for the grown ups. I was about to reach for my notebook, when I thought I heard the Pastor say my name.

I looked up and could see he was talking, but not looking at anyone in particular. Then, mid-sentence, he turned in my direction. Was he looking at me? Maybe he was just looking this way? I couldn't really understand what he was saying, but it was like the words were alive somehow, like the words he was saying from the bible were talking to me. It sounds weird even thinking about it. But ***I was almost sure I could hear a voice, in the words.***

But I don't even know what that means? It doesn't make sense. Anyway, this is too weird. Maybe it was what I ate for breakfast. Harry did make the scrambled eggs, and I only ate it to be nice.

. . .

After service on our way home, I thought about mentioning it to Aunt Eliza. Would she think I'm being silly? Just making things up?

CHAPTER 8

ANYONE FOR GREEN BANANA BREAD

It's been two weeks already. This holiday is whizzing by so quickly. Aunt Eliza took Harry, Patricia and I to London Zoo. It was our first major outing. Aunt Eliza asked which animal was my favourite, but I couldn't choose. I loved the Giraffes, the Zebra's, the otters, the penguins, the llama's and flamingos.

But now, the morning after, as I'm curled up still under the bedcovers at 10am thinking about it, my thoughts are drawn to the lions and lionesses I saw. I thought I would be scared of them. I mean, they were a bit scary, but there was something about them. Their piercing eyes that seem to look through me. They seemed fierce and protective at the same time.

It's so hard to get out of bed today. But then I realised I had promised to help Aunt Eliza bake dessert. I quickly washed and dressed, thank goodness Harry and Patricia were still asleep, no fighting for bathroom rights this morning. I ran downstairs as quickly as I could.

"Slow down, are you running to catch a train?" Aunt Eliza said. I giggled, "Morning Aunt Eliza". "Morning pumpkin, did you sleep well?" "I did. I wanted to watch... I mean, help you make the banana bread". "Well good thing I went to the supermarket to pick up the ingredients early this morning. Grab the yellow bananas, eggs and ground mixed spice for me. I'll get the sugar, oil and the loaf tin". I sensed some excitement in Aunt Eliza's voice.

"Close this side of the blinds please pumpkin, that light is hurting my eyes". I didn't think it was that bright, but I closed them anyway. I think Aunt Eliza would wear her sunglasses in the house if she could.

I looked on the shelves for mixed spice and in the fridge for the other items, but I couldn't see the ingredients. I double and triple check, but I couldn't see them! Aunt Eliza wouldn't make a mistake. I started to feel bad. I'm not being very helpful. Should have stayed in bed!

Ok, here goes. "Aunt Eliza, I can't see the yellow bananas, and there's no ground mixed spice in the cupboard, just salt, pepper and mixed herbs". "Child, what are you talking about? I bought those things this morning, let me see!"

Aunt Eliza rummaged in the pantry and the fridge. "Here!" She said, holding out a small bottle to my face. "What's this say? And here are the bananas!" Aunt Eliza pulled a bunch of bananas out and rested them on the table. I laughed teasingly, "Aunt Eliza, you're being silly. Those are green bananas and that's the mixed herbs," I smiled, looking back towards the fridge, expecting her to stop joking around and pull out the real thing.

She looked at me with a puzzled look. Then, as if she wasn't sure whether to laugh or scold me, but with a tone somewhere in between, she said "stop, stop laughing!"

Harry suddenly appeared at the kitchen door. Then tottered into the kitchen, half yawning. "What's so funny? What's for breakfast?" He said picking up the bananas. "And what are you making with these ingredients? Green bananas Mum! We're not having boiled food are we?" Harry moaned, scrunching up his face in disgust.

Aunt Eliza's face was a picture of worry and unease. When she caught me staring at her, she quickly changed her look. "Right! Harry upstairs, wash, dress, then come and make your breakfast. Sam, I'm not feeling up to making banana bread today, tell you what you can do for me; here is £5 pop to the corner shop and buy a nice madeira cake we can have for dessert later". Harry started moaning and I began to protest, but Aunt Eliza was having none of it from either of us.

Then Aunt Eliza's phone rang. "Harry, check who's ringing for me please?" With a puzzled look on his face Harry said, "the phone is right there Mum, can't you just check it?" Aunt Eliza shot him a look that said she was not in the mood for any mouthing off. Harry looked at the phone screen and said, "it's the doctor's surgery".

Aunt Eliza grabbed the phone from Harry and answered it, as she shuffled us both out the kitchen.

CHAPTER 9

POUTY FISH LIPS

WEEK THREE

It's the third week of what is supposed to be; 'The Best Summer Holiday Ever!' But, I'm just not so sure anymore. I'm just chilling on my bed, trying to process my thoughts and staring straight ahead of me at my, 'All that glitters isn't gold' poster. Hmmm.

I do love my god sister and brother, and they seem popular and very tech savvy. But the other day, they took my phone and created an Instagram account in my name and used the worst picture of me from my first night here as my profile picture. I can't believe they did that! They said it was a joke, but it wasn't funny.

. . .

Those two are always on their phones, they tell Aunt Eliza they are posting messages to provoke people to think about God and get them to think outside the box. What does that even mean? Where is God in all this? What box? Who's in a box?

Most of their posts have nothing to do with God. I've seen selfies of Patricia with these pouty fish lips and Harry looking down the camera lens as if he were taking one of those prisoner mugshots you see in films. As for their videos, I just don't get them. There's no real message or even context to any of them. The majority of them feature Patricia filming herself, doing some of the most mundane tasks and talking about everything and nothing all at the same time. I'm not sure if they're supposed to be funny or thought-provoking.

I don't want to judge them, because maybe I'm just too young to understand. I suppose it's just their way of having fun. But the thoughts and feelings lingered in my mind for a while. Then, like a bad dream, flashing from scene to scene, I had this sense of things going from bad to worse, the intensity was building but more so the feeling, a bad feeling, a weight... AHHH IT'S TOO MUCH.

I jumped up and shook myself, to try and shake off the feeling. I tried to just ignore it but then I thought about what the Youth Pastor had said: "Write it down and ask God what it means and who it's for?"

. . .

I grabbed my journal and wrote down what I had been thinking and feeling about the twins for the last three weeks, exactly halfway through my trip. I wrote about how my excitement to meet them and be accepted by them, had turned into sadness and disappointment. I wrote and wrote about them laughing at me, the name calling, doing things behind my back and how hard it is choosing between being accepted by THEM or doing the right thing, even if that meant being on my own sometimes.

I stopped writing. Sat back, and stared beyond my poster... Suddenly the words; 'Social Media' ***really impressed on me.***

What does it mean? Is God trying to say something to me about; 'Social Media' or is it for someone else? And why tell me? Why not Aunt Eliza? What on earth can I do about it?

So, I prayed;

"Lord, if you are speaking to me, please make this message clear. If I need to do something or warn someone, please give me clarity and courage. In Jesus name, Amen".

CHAPTER 10

A CONVERSATION WITH GOD

WEEK FOUR

It's 7:20am and I think it's Wednesday, I chuckle to myself. Why do I always forget what day it is during the summer holidays?

Sitting on the floor in my room, staring into the gorgeous tall oval mirror. How shall I wear my hair today? Ponytail? Bunches? Or leave my curls out? I could try plaiting it, but the last time I did, Patricia said I looked like a sensa fowl. I thought she was being nice until Harry showed me a picture of it on his phone. I couldn't believe she'd compared me to a chicken with uneven ruffled feathers. I know she teases a lot, it's just her way. I can have a good laugh at myself, but sometimes, I don't know if she is laughing with me or at me.

. . .

Aunt Eliza on the other hand, is always kind! She's always saying how smart and pretty I am, and that I remind her of her when she was a little girl.

As I stand up, still looking in the mirror, I decide to pull my hair up in one (just like Aunt Eliza does when she's at home). I wonder if I will look like her when I grow up. Our hair is the same and our skin tone is similar. I close my eyes pretending I'm her, and try to mimic her voice. Lost in character, I see myself in an Aunt Eliza outfit, in Church on a Sunday, sharing one of her famous words of encouragement as she does every week. I'm holding a microphone, I take to the stage... I'm suddenly snapped out of it, by what I thought was a loud banging noise outside my door. I check to see if Harry and Patricia are okay, but they are still snoring away, dead to the world.

I race down the stairs to check on Aunt Eliza when I hear her voice. Is she on the phone I wonder? As I gingerly make my way down the last few steps and edge towards the living room door, I hear her. I realise she's praying. I think about walking away, but then I'm curious to hear how she talks to God, and if God talks back.

One more step closer and I can now hear Aunt Eliza's words; "But Lord, I'm trying my best with these children. I don't know how they've gotten so out of hand. But I know they'll come good in their own time, it's just a phase, they're not bad children".

Pause

"God, I know you've spoken to me before…"

Pause

"It's not that I'm being short sighted…"

Pause

"I'm not making excuses for them, well maybe I am. You know best, Father".

Pause. Aunt Eliza is nodding and sniffling.

"I really pray things don't get worse. God surely, it's not that bad. I don't want to be too hard on them. I'm all they have since their father died. I can't bring myself to…."

"I don't want them to hurt more than they already are..."

As I listened, it sounded like God really cared about Aunt Eliza. Is she worried about the twins? I've noticed they can push the boundaries. Again, that uneasy, almost sick feeling in my stomach, (or is it in my chest?) Feels like something bad is going to happen. I hope God gives Aunt Eliza the courage to do the right thing.

At that moment the doorbell rang. I heard Aunt Eliza getting up from her knees, so I raced up the stairs, just far enough to be out of sight, but within ear shot. As I heard the door open, a pleasant, warm, almost singsong voice came flooding into the house.

. . .

"Eliza, I was knocking on the door earlier didn't you hear?"

"Joyce, good to see you is everything alright?"

"I just had to stop by and tell you. Have you heard about Brother Dennis? You know how he's getting on in age, well he had a fall and they had to rush him to A&E. Thank goodness his niece, you remember she's a nurse, well, she went to check in on him by chance and found him, otherwise he could have been lying there all night!"

"Is he doing okay Joyce?"

"Oh yes, yes nothing broken thank goodness, just a bit sore and bruised. But the hospital is keeping him in for observation. Apparently, he's keeping the ward entertained with his jokes and stories".

"Well, that is good news, I mean, that it wasn't serious. Are you and your family well Joyce? How's Terry and Rochelle?"

"Well, that's what I wanted to tell you. The other day I was talking to my friend Maxine and she was telling me that her half-sister Janelle found out her daughter Melissa had been using what they call a decoy app on her phone. She had been sending inappropriate text messages to this boy she thought was from school, for two months, her Mum was none the wiser". Joyce's voice went from melodic to almost shrill as she expressed her surprise.

"What?" Said Aunt Eliza. "How did she find out?"

"She just happened to catch the last ten minutes of some programme where they talked about this app. Their daughter had been acting a bit out of the ordinary for a while but the parents couldn't figure out why the change in behaviour, they thought it was just teenage hormones".

"Okay, wow, but Joyce, you're telling me this because?" Aunt Eliza's voice started to sound a bit impatient.

"Well, I'm telling everyone Eliza, you know me. I know your two can be a bit of a handful at times and teenagers will be teenagers you know".

"Joyce!" Aunt Eliza's voice sounded unusually snappish. "I appreciate the call, but my kids are not a handful!"

"Now, I didn't mean it like that". Joyce sounded remorseful.

"I know you didn't, but they're good kids, they just need time that's all".

"Oh of course, how long has it been now? A year!" Joyce said, her voice sounding more apologetic.

"Yes, well I have to go now Joyce, I have an appointment at the hairdressers and if I don't leave now…"

I could just about see Aunt Eliza closing the door as she spoke. "Oh yes dear alright, God bless. Bye".

Aunt Eliza closed the door with a little more force than I think she intended. Then I heard her say "I know my children. No one knows them better than me!"

She picked up her bag and shouted upstairs. "Children I've left a note on the table for you. I'm just popping out; I'll be about an hour". Then she picked up her keys and headed out the door.

CHAPTER 11

THE UNINTENTIONAL DETECTIVE

WEEK FIVE

I'm missing Mum and Dad. I speak to them every day but when they called my mobile phone this morning, it's like, somehow, they knew I needed to hear their voices.

I told them I was fine, and they asked me how I was getting on with the twins. What I wanted to say was; "the twins are becoming so annoying and they aren't helping out Aunt Eliza as much as they should", but all I actually said was, "I'm fine, we're getting along, fine".

"Make sure you do as Aunt Eliza tells you," instructed Mum. "And remember Sam, you're a leader not a follower!" Dad rehearsed. "We love you and give your Aunt Eliza a hug from us," they both chorused as they hung up the phone.

As I sat on the edge of the bed, I could hear Harry and Patricia talking, they think they can whisper, but they can't! It sounded like Patricia was annoying Harry as usual. Something about Harry sleeping his holidays away and Patricia going to the park with friends. I decided to get up and join in the conversation, but as I approached to knock on Harry's door, I overheard:

"Come on Harry. I'll call Chris, Amanda and Dwayne to meet up with us with the rum," Patricia said. "As long as they're not going to be messing with cars again this time. Plus, you're never going to be allowed out the house without Mum asking you to take Sam with you. Sam won't fit in with this crowd," said Harry. "I'm not Sam's babysitter! Anyway, don't worry, I'll get the money from Mum's purse for their cigarettes and then we'll sneak out. Harry we'll literally be an hour, Mum won't even notice!" Patricia plotted.

I slid back into my room to remain unseen. Babysitter!! I felt offended. I'm not a baby, I'm almost eleven! Well, I wasn't in the mood for going out today anyway!

I heard Harry and Patricia making their way downstairs to speak to Aunt Eliza, probably to make up some lie about where they were going and why I couldn't come.

. . .

I could feel myself starting to sulk, when suddenly, I felt a strong feeling, an impression maybe, to go into Harry's room. I tried to ignore it, but the feeling got stronger. I checked to see if they were coming back upstairs, but I could hear them both in full flow of conversation.

I slowly stepped into his room. I could see messages pinging on both of their phones. Harry's phone was on his desk and Patricia's was on the bed. As I looked back and forth at their phones, the comments popping up from their social media feeds, I could not believe my eyes. This didn't look good. This didn't feel good. What had these two got into?

"There is no way Aunt Eliza could know about this," I said out loud. Then I quickly cupped my hand over my mouth realising I spoke my thoughts out loud.

I picked up Patricia's phone, it got worse, the nasty name calling wasn't just what she was doing to me, she was doing it to others online; name calling, belittling and posting horrible images of people, comparing them to all sorts of animals and monster like movie characters. But the worst, was a most recent post about a young person from church, who had shared a personal struggle and was looking for advice. She had shamed him online!

. . .

WAIT… WHAT? A side-by-side photo of me and a sensa fowl, with the caption, 'guess which one's my god sister Samantha?' I dropped the phone, burst into tears and ran to my room.

I need to tell Aunt Eliza.

But how would I explain being in their rooms and looking at the twin's phones? Everyone will know it was me. The twins will never speak to me again. Aunt Eliza will think I can't be trusted. It's not worth the hassle. And what would Harry and Patricia do to me? I don't want to upset Aunt Eliza, she's got enough to deal with. But she needs to know. Oh God this is so hard.

CHAPTER 12

IN THE GARDEN ROOM

I needed to be by myself. So, I went out back to the garden, ok it's more like a field, lol. Aw, it actually felt nice to smile in the midst of all this madness.

Gosh this garden is perfectly, neat and tidy. The twins are more interested in their stupid phones than spending time in nature. Aunt Eliza comes out every morning during the summer to have, what she calls, "her coffee with God". Other times she will be out trimming her flowers. Now and again I'll see the local gardener but other than that, no-one comes out here, so I like to call this, my other room.

This is a picture-perfect garden; seating area, freshly mowed grass and the most beautiful flowers; roses, lily's, sunflowers and my favourite peonies. Well, actually, they're my Mum's favourite but she doesn't mind me copying.

All the flowers have their section and every time I'm out here; I appreciate the beauty more and more.

The peonies make me smile. Every single time I look at them, I say in my head; "Mum would LOVE these," and I smile, like it's the very first time I'm having the thought. This time I'm stopped in my tracks! Something's wrong, out of place, different. What are those sorry looking flowers in the midst of the beautiful peony's?

A beautiful ring of peony flowers and two sorry looking flowers right in the centre. I wonder if Aunt Eliza will notice and cut them off? They're ruining the beauty. Mum wouldn't be impressed; she'd cut them off without a second thought!

Another thing I love to do in the garden, aka, my other room, is lay on the springy grass and look up at the sky. This summer hasn't been super-hot, so being outside is much more bearable than it was last summer.

Dad and I love to look up at the clouds and name what we see. When I do this, sitting in Aunt Eliza's garden, I think of all the silly things he would be saying about what he sees in the sky.

Today as I looked up, I noticed a cloud, ***one dark cloud***. The rest of the sky was a bright, brilliant blue, completing the rainbow of colours in my eye-line; brightly painted colourful houses against the blue-sky background. There was a scatter of white clouds here and there but mainly blue sky. So, this one dark cloud was so out of place, it didn't make any sense, would it just rain in one place? Where did the cloud even come from? Was it connected to another set of clouds? My thoughts make me sit up right with concern, that maybe this little cloud was a sign... of rain?

A rustle from the large tree in the back of the garden caught my attention. How unusual to see an Aspen tree with ***some of its leaves still golden-yellow***. I shivered; the gentle breeze was feeling a little too cool. The tree shimmered it's gorgeous gold leaves, just as I decided to head inside.

"Such a beautiful gold tree," I said to myself as I approached the back door of the house. Then I turned to look at the tree again, it's gold but not... I gasped and cupped my hands over my mouth as though I could stop the thought. This is all so weird, or should I say interesting, coincidental? Wait every time I say coincidence, I can hear our Bishop's voice in my head; *"there are no coincidences in God!"*

CHAPTER 13

PUZZLE PIECES

WEEK SIX

All that glitters isn't gold...
All that glitters isn't gold...
All that glitters isn't gold...

Why does this theme keep coming up everywhere?? Maybe this is how God speaks to me?

What was it the Youth Pastor said to do? Oh yes, I should write down what I wanted to say to God, ask Him to speak to me when I read the Bible and ask Him who the message is for. Then he said something about... oh what was the other thing he said. That's it, ***God speaks through a verse of the Bible or some words or a picture.***

. . .

I raced upstairs and logged onto Aunt Eliza's computer to look up the meaning of glitter.

G-L-I-T-T-E-R I hit the return key and up popped the definition:

An attractive and exciting but superficial quality.

Hmm, attractive but superficial. What could that relate to? I tried to connect the dots, but I couldn't think what it could mean.

Then I looked up gold and it said:

A precious metal used especially in jewellery.

Huh! Mum and Aunt Eliza only wear real gold jewellery, Mum always says; 'If it's not real, it shows after time'. But I remember the teacher saying something in school, that precious things aren't shallow but found deep within the earth.

I got up from the computer and paced the floor trying to put it all together. This is like a puzzle, I thought.

. . .

You like puzzles Sam. Where do you always start. With the most obvious pieces first.

I scrolled on my phone and found the picture of the poster on my wall. It can't be a coincidence!

I sat back at the computer and typed in the phrase:

"All that glitters is not gold" and held my breath.

Up popped the definition:

The attractive external appearance of something is not a reliable indication of its true nature.

Not its true nature. I said the words slowly, to, myself.

Okay Sam, what do we have here?

1. Glitter is exciting but superficial
2. Gold is something precious
3. The phrase means not its true nature.

Suddenly my mind was flooded with all the signs that I dismissed over the last few weeks. The poster, Dad said the same phrase the first night we spoke, and the signs in nature.

. . .

I sunk into the chair and closed my eyes. When I opened them the screen saver on Aunt Eliza's computer was a picture of her standing with Patricia and Harry. A heavy troubled feeling came over me. I switched off the computer and ran to my room.

I know Harry and Patricia miss their Dad, but they're trying to fill that gap with the wrong things.

"God!" I prayed, "Please help Aunt Eliza. Keep Harry and Patricia safe and help them make better choices".

I climbed into bed, my heart racing but then, like a blanket, a sense of calm came over me, it's the last week of my holiday. And with that thought I drifted off to sleep.

CHAPTER 14

IT'S THE POLICE!

THE LAST NIGHT

"Harry! Patricia!" I heard Aunt Eliza shouting from downstairs. She seemed really distressed.

"Sam! Are Harry and Patricia upstairs? I was sure I left my purse and keys in the living room".

I paused my packing and headed down the stairs into the lounge where Aunt Eliza was rummaging through her bag, searching the tabletops, the floors and between the chair cushions. She did not seem herself, a bit on edge. Should I say something?

. . .

"Aunt Eliza, I'll help you look, don't worry we'll find it," I said trying to pacify her concern also, my own. She then said, almost under her breath, "I've got a bad feeling about them two..."

Her words and her frantic searching were interrupted by five hard knocks at the door. We both shot each other an instant look of concern. "Go answer the door Sam!" Aunt Eliza said with a hint of concern in her voice.

I hastily moved to the door, feeling really lightheaded. "Who is it?" I questioned, faintly making out Harry and Patricia's body shapes through the frosted windowpane in the door. But if it was them, surely, they'd use their key?

The answer that returned almost made me pass out. "IT'S THE POLICE!!" What... I didn't open the door; I lowered my hand from the handle and took 3 steps backwards and said almost in tears, "It's the Police Aunt Eliza!"

She walked towards me, staring at me like I did something wrong. She stepped past me and opened the door.

Standing there was Harry, Patricia, and two Police Officers.

. . .

"Hello, Officers!" Aunt Eliza said with a smile that looked like a child had painted it onto her face. While shooting Harry and Patricia the sharpest look, then back to her fake smile to the Officers.

"Good Afternoon Mrs…" the Officer started. "Oh, please call me Eliza. What happened?" "Well Eliza," the Officer continued, "we found them hanging around with a group of youths we know to cause trouble in the area. We've been keeping an eye on them and noticed these two. They didn't seem to fit in with that crowd, so we thought we'd better intervene and bring them home, before they got in over their heads, if you know what I mean".

"Thank you, I really appreciate that. So sorry to cause you any trouble. What happens now?" "Well, if having a lot to say for yourself was an offence we'd have this young lady up for charges, but they weren't doing anything wrong, so the matter is closed. But perhaps a good talking might be in order?"

As Harry and Patricia came into the house, heads hung low, Aunt Eliza closed the door AND LET RIP!

"How dare you!" She shouted. "How could you!" She waved her hands in despair. "You lied to me about where you were going, and you let Police come to my door! You're an embarrassment to me, both of you…"

She was interrupted by her phone, which she held straight up to my face and demanded, "who is it Sam? I can't even see I'm so angry!" "It says Pastor," I reply sheepishly.

"Greetings Pastor, how are you? Can I… What? They did what? Um, it was definitely them? Of course. I am so sorry. Ok, Ok. Today… No tomorrow, no problem, we'll be there. Ok see you at 9am sharp. Again, I am so sorry!!" She hung up and turned, ever so slowly towards the twins.

"Cyber… Bullying…" Aunt Eliza said slowly, then looked away and paused, trying to gather her thoughts and form her words.

"I can't even LOOK at you two right now. Tomorrow morning at 9am we have to go and see Pastor because you have been accused of Cyberbullying. And I'm supposed to be going to the airport to pick up Sam's parents and take them all home. My eyes hurt, my head hurts. The Police just brought you home, NOW THIS. It's too much. OH GOD WHY! What do you have to say for yourselves???"

. . .

Patricia jumps in with not a shred of remorse "Mum we were just…"

"YOU WERE JUST… I don't even want to hear it right now. Give me your phones and GET TO YOU ROOMS... NOW!!"

Aunt Eliza takes their phones and turns her face out of my eye line. I quickly leave the room to give her space and as I follow the twins out the door. I can't believe my eyes; Patricia has just snuck Aunt Eliza's keys and purse back onto the side table in the hallway. Am I in a movie?

CHAPTER 15

ELIZA THE AUNT'S NEED FOR SPEED

THE LAST NIGHT

I know in stories and movies the 'good' always triumphs over the 'bad' in the end, but it feels like reality just doesn't match-up.

It's 8:40am, just passed my packed bags in the hallway, ready to finally head home later. Now I'm sitting in the front seat of the car, beside a woman that to me, is more like an angel than an everyday citizen. It's just not fair that the negative presence of her children in the back of the car has somehow cast a dark cloud over everything.

How can you be happy and experience joy, when you're sat in the middle of a storm? How does Aunt Eliza do this day after day? She loves these two desperately and they've barely said a word to her all morning. I mean this whole thing is their fault! They wouldn't be this tired if they hadn't stayed up until 3 o'clock this morning being silly.

How disrespectful can you get? The Police come to the house, reprimand your mother, you get sent to your rooms and you still stay up all night acting the fool and being loud.

I'll never forget overhearing Mum speaking once about; 'it not being right that a certain person was overcompensating and allowing their children to get away with all sorts because their father had died.' I always wondered who she was talking about, but now I know. She was talking about Aunt Eliza.

Why would they behave this way? Why would they bring problems to their mothers' door? She clearly loves them so much and gives them everything they asked for. The least they could do is just give her a little love back. She must feel so sad. To have lost the love of her husband and both her children, all around the same time. This must be heart-breaking.

I turn and look at Aunt Eliza and my heart aches. How did somebody so good end up with a set of children who are so… so... so.... 'not good'.

. . .

As I sit here and gaze over at Aunt Eliza, she's starting to look so different to me. That sparkle in her eye that always made her look like she was shining, is now starting to look so different. Those shiny reflective surfaces in her eyes, aren't the unique feature of somebody who has the eyes of an angel. I see it now; I see it so clearly. They're tears. Tears that just won't flow. Tears that have taken up residence and are just always there.

Aunt Eliza glances over in my direction, not quite looking at me but out the window. She attempts a half smile, which feels as though it's aimed at me, but all I can see when I look at her now are the year-old tears, doing their dance around her grey tinted pupil.

Aunt Eliza is special, and she deserves to be treated with so much more respect. I'll tell you just how special she is... God made each and every one of us so different. Different skin colour, hair colour, eye colour and appearance. With that said though, there is one thing He gave us that's the same. We all have black pupils in our eyes. No matter what colour our iris, our pupils are black. But Aunt Eliza is different. God blessed her with one grey pupil (or glittering silver if you look really closely) and that seals the deal for me. She is somebody very special.

When she smiles, her eyes start to sparkle, it's the most beautiful sight. But today, the sparkle is just so dull. She hasn't smiled once, not properly anyway. Her half smiles have appeared every now and again, more as a check-in with me, to make sure that I'm okay.

She woke us all up at 8am this morning, which during the summer holidays feels like torture. The visit from the police last night has clearly shaken her up and the talk of cyberbullying hasn't helped. We're going somewhere in South London to meet with the church Pastor and some other important sounding people. The twins don't seem too bothered, but the speed at which she made us leave the house, makes me feel really nervous.

I had never heard Aunt Eliza raise her voice before yesterday. So, hearing her yell, "GET IN THE CAR!" before she slammed the front door shut this morning, has still got my heart racing. We were in such a rush that we didn't eat breakfast and I NEVER miss breakfast. I'm not sure if it was intentional or if Aunt Eliza just forgot, but it just doesn't seem like a good time to say anything.

She commanded me to sit in the front seat with such authority I just jumped in. Even though the way she told me didn't feel great, I love getting the opportunity to sit in the front seat. You get to focus on what's ahead of you and take in the amazing view of the world around you.

. . .

Aunt Eliza forgets to turn the airbag off, a ritual for Dad and I whenever I sit in the front seat of his car. Today, skipping the ritual makes me feel like an adult. I could remind Aunt Eliza, but the twins will probably smirk at each other and make me feel like a little girl. I contemplate saying something for about a second then think… nah! I feel like an adult riding in the front seat, airbag on. This is the life.

The speed at which Aunt Eliza is driving this car has something inside me feeling a little on edge. I've never had such an uncomfortable car journey in all my ten years, eleven months and twenty-nine days. If there wasn't so much tension in the car, I'd probably make a little joke about her being a race car driver in disguise. I can hear the fast-paced race commentators voice in my head now... *"and in the lead we have Eliza the Aunt, she swerves from left to right with great precision and control, Eliza the Aunt is in the lead as she approaches the left turn. Oooh she turns in a little bit early and..."*

"WAIT, AUNT ELIZA, LOOK OUT!!!"

CHAPTER 16

THE LIVESTREAM SAM WISHED WAS A DREAM

THE LAST FEW HOURS

I've watched ambulances speed past me in the street so many times and they've always seemed so cool. The bright flashing blue lights furiously commanding the attention of everybody nearby. The sound of the blaring sirens filling every ounce of the air. And the speed - just wow. I always figured those lightning speed journeys must be so much fun.

Well, let's put it this way, I found out today that I figured wrong! There is always a reason they command the respect of everybody en route, and the reason is usually because somebody is near death. They have a vehicle filled with hurt, anxiety and uncertainty, not cool at all.

. . .

Today I qualified to experience one of those, not-so-cool journeys in an ambulance. I now know what it feels like to have a body filled with adrenaline, fear and pain all at the same time, and I don't ever want to feel like this again.

I'm so sore from my face-to-face meeting with the passenger side airbag in Aunt Eliza's car. My position, in the front seat was supposed to be punishment to the twins, but now, somehow, it feels like I drew the short straw and have been punished more than them. Once again, it feels like the good guy is suffering. Why can't us 'good guys' get a break?

That soft, lovely, slow-motion, caress of a beautiful bag of air that I'd always seen in television test crashes, is not at all the reality of this situation. Dad allows me to sit in the front seat of his car but always opens the glove box first to turn the airbag off. He always explains that the beautiful bag of air would hurt a small child, so he had to turn it off to keep me safe. I never understood how he could turn off a 'safety feature' to protect me, it made no sense. I was nearly 11 now, I wasn't a small child anymore.

The revelation of that routine has hit me as hard as the airbag hit my face. My Grandma always used to say in her beautiful Jamaican accent; *"who don't hear must feel!"* And boy was I feeling it now.

. . .

I still can't fully comprehend what happened. One moment we're driving and I'm staring at my beautiful Aunt Eliza, as she manoeuvres the car across the streets of South London, the next moment, I open my eyes and Harry is pulling me out of a car shouting. "WAKE-UP!"

"What just happened, what is it, what, what?" I stutter in an obvious state of confusion. Nobody's answering me.

I turn back and look in the car. My heart feels like it breaks instantly as I glimpse Aunt Eliza still inside the vehicle, motionless. She's lying lifeless over her airbag covered steering wheel, not saying anything, not blinking, not moving, just nothing.

I gasp, and without even having the time to schedule my tears, they begin to flow down my face with such order, speed and precision, it's hard to tell one tear from the next.

It's been a tough summer and I've had moments of great sadness, but for the first time, I whisper quietly to myself, "I just want my Mum and Dad".

As soon as the words leave my mouth, I feel a warm heavy hand squeeze my shoulder. I take a deep breath, "Dad?" I whisper so quietly not even I hear the word. I turn around as fast as I can to be greeted by a tall, solid framed man who isn't my Dad at all. Instead, I see a tall, broad-shouldered, pale skinned man. He looks like the kind of man my Dad would be friends with. His green eyes were so bright and even though very different from my Dad's, they had the same caring, compassionate glance as my Dad's. I could see his concern. What did he see when he looked at me?

I touched my face to make sure I wasn't bleeding, but as fast as my hand arrived to my cheek, THE PAIN that surged through my body forced me to throw my hands out to the side as far away from my face as they could go. "Are you OK young lady?" He asked, visibly concerned.

How do I even answer that question? I'm hurt, I'm scared, I'm confused but all I can say is, "Yes". 'Yes... YES...' What I am saying? I suddenly understand why the Shunamite woman in 2 Kings in the Bible was able to say; 'it is well' when Gehazi asked her how she was. I've never been able to understand how she didn't blurt out "my son is dead, I'm tired, I'm scared, and I really need your help". I kinda get it now.

The man places one hand on each of my shoulders, crouches down and begins speaking. "My name is Kevin and I'm a paramedic. You've just been involved in a car accident. I'm going to take you into the ambulance so I can..."

. . .

I just took his lead and walked with him. I stopped hearing what he was saying. 'I was just involved in a car accident'... What? How? Just huh?

As I took a step up to enter the ambulance, I suddenly remembered Aunt Eliza and the twins. I glanced back to see two paramedics using all their strength to get Aunt Eliza lifted onto a stretcher. I searched her face for a sign that she might be OK, but my search returned a result that said; 'Unfortunately we cannot find what you are looking for'.

I quickly scanned the scene to look for the twins and I couldn't believe what I saw. Patricia stood there with her phone in hand (the phone that got confiscated last night may I add) taking a selfie of herself sandwiched between the now concertina shaped metal crushed car bonnet and her mother being pushed away on a stretcher.

Then there was Harry. Harry just looked so confused. He too stood in the middle of two very different things. He gazed longingly and concerned at his mother being pushed towards the ambulance but looked back at his sister with a similar look of concern. I could read him like a book. He wanted to be with his Mum, I saw it in his eyes. But he also cared a great deal about what his sister would think of him if he ran to join his Mum.

. . .

There was a loud bang as the stretcher made contact with the ambulance step which made me jump. Kevin was checking my heartbeat, eyesight and whatever else he was checking as I watched the paramedics push my beautiful Angelic Aunt Eliza in front of me. I just wanted to grab her, shake her and wake her up. She must be asleep, that's all. Just having a little sleep.

Another paramedic was behind Harry and Patricia, escorting them onto the ambulance. I could tell by the way the three paramedics were glancing at each other that they were horrified by the behaviour of the twins. Harry had chosen his sister! They were laughing and joking as though they had just come off the most exciting fun-filled rollercoaster ride of their lives.

Harry cared about his Mum; I know he did. I saw it in his face when he had seen his Mum being rolled towards the ambulance on a stretcher. So why was he behaving like this? What a shame!

We rushed through the streets at what felt like 100mph and as if God had given the vehicle a serious instruction... 'Don't slow down, don't greet any stop signs, don't stop in any traffic, JUST KEEP GOING!'

. . .

The voices around me felt muffled. I couldn't comprehend anything. "Come on Aunt Eliza please wake up!" I thought, "just open your eyes and wake-up!"

My gaze was switching between this beautiful lady laying right in front of me on a stretcher and her two children that found it appropriate to be streaming live to their social media pages. I may have been the youngest child on that ambulance, but I knew I was the wisest. What a disappointment these two were.

Before I knew it, we were at the hospital. As I stepped off the ambulance, I realised how bad the current situation was and how 'not good' Aunt Eliza's children really were.

CHAPTER 17

GOD OF THE IMPOSSIBLE

"We'll call you and you can just tell us where you are"

"We'll CALL you and you can just tell us where you are"

"We'll call YOU and YOU can JUST"

"JUST"

Are these two for real?

We are in a state of emergency and they are thinking about their stomachs. Hungry? Gift shop? Seriously?

There are paramedics running around us, people shouting big words at each other and these two jokers are talking about food. I'm done. I am so done with them. I'm not even gonna respond.

. . .

I get escorted to a small waiting room by a lovely lady. She's a nurse, young, wearing a very close fitted uniform and her hair is slicked back not a strand out of place. She looks about twenty, there is something about her that makes me want to be her friend.

She asks me if I'm okay, but the words just won't come. She asks if I need anything, but my mouth won't open. She tells me she'll sit with me for a while, so we sit there, together, in silence.

I admit it felt a little awkward, but my words had just left me. I was in total shock. What on earth was going on? Why was I here and not sat praying for those two rebellious teens at their Pastors house?

The lovely nurse then takes a phone out of her pocket and asks me what music I'm into. It's at that point I utter the first six words I'd spoken in hours. "I want my Mum and Dad."

I don't remember if she told me her name and I know I didn't ask for it. What I do know for sure though, is that she was amazing! I'd forgotten that I had my own phone safely tucked away in my jeans pocket. Before I knew it, my phone was in my hand with Dad's number on the screen. I heard a few rings, then, Dad's calming, familiar voice saying, "Sam-Sam Baby-girl, how you doing?"

With that I burst into tears and again my words left me. My nurse (I call her that affectionately because at that moment it felt like God had placed her there just for me) was amazing. She took the phone and told my Dad EVERYTHING. As she spoke, she answered questions for me that I didn't even know I had.

Aunt Eliza had turned the car too early into a side road while we were driving. She'd clearly misjudged it and as a result had ran into a tree stump and crashed the car.

My nurse told my Dad that nobody had been seriously hurt, and that he should try not to panic. With this statement, I just held her hand and squeezed it. Everything was going to be alright.

She told Dad that, even though Aunt Eliza was in a slight state of shock, she was alright. During her 'pre-admission assessment' (she kept referring to that bit as Triage) a nurse had checked her eyes to make sure her pupils were responsive. This is when they found a cataract covering her left eye.

. . .

HOLD ON A MINUTE... her left eye. Her beautiful glittering silver pupil. What was she saying? The thing about my Aunt Eliza that I thought was a beautiful, unique feature of hers, was actually not beautiful at all. It was destructive and dangerous.

All that glitters really isn't gold, wow!

She told Dad a few more bits of information I didn't fully understand, mentioned the twins had gone AWOL, then handed me back the phone.

The calming feature of Dad's voice had changed so drastically, and I heard his serious, 'Pastor-Dad' voice this time round. "Sam, are you there?" he remarked, with such authority it made me sit up straight. "I'm here Daddy," I replied.

"Listen Sam, this is a time for you to be strong. God never gives us more than we can handle, so know you can handle this". I really wasn't expecting that to be the first thing he said to me. I sat a little straighter and listened with increasing curiosity regarding where this conversation would lead.

"Sam, I need you to be strong. If not for you, for your Aunt Eliza. Our flight is the next flight back to the UK, so there's no way we can get to you any faster. As soon as we land, we'll make our way straight to the hospital. The nurse just told me they are going to let you sit with your Aunt in a little while and that you should be able to stay with her until we get there. Now dig deep, find your strength and use it for both you and your Aunt. Your Mum wants to speak to you. Stay strong and I'll see you soon. I love you Baby girl".

Before I could finish saying, "I love you too Daddy," I heard the soft soothing tone of Mum's voice, which made me push the phone a little closer to my ear.

"Sam Honey, I want you to pray with your Aunt Eliza when you get in the room. Pray, asking God for your heart's desire for your Aunt. God will hear you, and answer your prayer". She paused but I could just feel that there was something else coming, so I sat quietly and just listened.

"You're sitting in the middle of St Thomas' hospital in London. I love that place so much because it's the same place you were born Sam. I always think of you when I hear the name of that hospital, because I didn't ever think I'd be blessed with a child that would call me Mummy".

At this point I heard my Mum sniffle, as if she were crying or desperately fighting back tears. I knew she was speaking from her heart now, and I felt a warm presence and goose bumps as she spoke.

"You see, I got told from a very young age that I couldn't have a baby. They refer to women whose bodies are unable to have children as 'infertile'. I know that's a term they use but every time I heard that word it hurt Sam. That label bothered me so much. I also got told from a young age in church that God can do the impossible. Now, thinking about my situation, these were two very different pieces of information. So, I decided to believe the Lord's report and not the medical profession. I asked God for a child".

Mum continued, "I prayed, and I prayed for a beautiful healthy baby. Every time I went back to the doctors, they reported that there was no chance it could happen. It was 'impossible', they told me. Every time I heard that word 'impossible' it made me pray a little harder to the 'God of the impossible'. I don't need to tell you how my story ended because I'm speaking to you today".

"Sam". Mum's voice changed, "God can do all things! Sometimes we just have to ask Him with sincere belief that He can and will do it".

. . .

"The doctors are saying that your Aunt is fine, but her eyesight has deteriorated so much that she may never see clearly again. Sam, that is their report, but like I just showed you, prayer can change things princess".

I'm pretty sure Mum hadn't finished speaking but I had to stop her. "Mum, thank you. I know what I have to do. Love you, bye".

Somehow, I heard Mum smile, then say, "I love you too my princess, see you soon".

With a smile on my face, I ended the call, feeling ten feet taller than I had when it started.

CHAPTER 18

THE SALVATION PRAYER

I wiped my damp cheek with the back of my hand, took one more deep breath, then said, "Gospel". My nurse hadn't taken her eyes off me since she handed the phone to me. She'd been looking at me reassuringly the whole time, but my speech had clearly baffled her.

"What was that sweetheart? I didn't quite catch what you said." I repeated "Gospel. I'm into gospel music".

With that she seemed to breathe a slight sigh of relief followed by a little giggle. "Well, it looks like I'm about to learn a thing or two about gospel music because I have no clue where to start".

. . .

My nurse and I sat waiting for the doctors to call me in to see Aunt Eliza for what felt like a whole day, but realistically, it was only about an hour. We played all my favourite gospel songs, spoke about the lyrics and didn't stop talking. No awkward silence, a slight injection of laughter and a whole lot of talk about Jesus.

When a doctor finally came to let My Nurse know that I could go and see Aunt Eliza, I could feel in the room we were both a little sad that our time together had ended. As the door slammed shut behind the doctor the words; "Can I pray with you?" Just flew out of my mouth. I shocked myself. I'd never done that before. What would I pray for? Mum asked me to pray with Aunt Eliza not the hospital staff.

My heart rate started increasing and I prepared to serve her an excuse she could use if she didn't want me to. Our mouths opened at the same time, as if our words were preparing to start a race. Her words won, as she uttered, "I'd really like that".

A wave of relief filled my body, but the nerves and anxiety were still there. I stood up next to her, placed my hand on her shoulder then started to pray, I praised God for being an awesome God, told Him that I really wanted to do his work, thanked Him for everything He had blessed us with, and said sorry for anything I'd done that would have disappointed Him. I thanked God for My Nurse's life and for our meeting today. I told God how wonderful she was and thanked Him for giving her such a large heart and for loving her so much.

I was forced to stop. I felt her body trembling in my hand. I had to open my eyes to make sure she was okay.

"Did I say something wrong?" I said with great concern. Through her tears, I heard, "No, no, I'm so sorry. It's just you said that God loves me and..." The tears were now streaming down her cheeks uncontrollably. Her hands were like windscreen wipers during a rainstorm. As fast as she wiped away the tears another influx would make a visit to her cheeks.

"He does love you. So much". I told her, sitting back down in the chair next to her, so I could have a better view of her face.

"I don't deserve it. I'm not a very nice person," she responded quickly as if she were trying to get me to stop talking.

"Jesus died for you. Surely that's enough evidence to prove how much He loves you".

"I know. I've been told that before. You're so matter of fact when you speak. It's so cute, but you wouldn't understand sweetie". With that she looked down at the floor as if she had been totally defeated by her thoughts.

"I don't need to understand!" I blurted out, trying to inject some authority into my voice.

"No matter what it is you feel you have done to be labelled 'not nice' all you have to do is say sorry. Say sorry, tell Jesus that you know He died for you, that you know He loves you, and that you want to let Him into your life" (Let's just call that Sam's version of The Salvation Prayer*).

After another brief moment of silence, I said, "would you pray with me? I'll finish mine, then you can say one of your own." She smiled at me and shook her head side to side, "I can't believe I'm saying this, but yes, I'll pray with you Sam".

I finished my prayer, said amen and was about to open my eyes when I heard:

"Dear God. Thank you for Sam, thank you for sending her to tell me that you love me. I'm really sorry for all the wrongs I've done. I really want to change; I need to change. I need you in my life. Help me to be more like Sam. Ummm, Amen".

She knew my name. But how? Maybe Mum or Dad had used it when she was speaking to them.

I feel amazing. My nurse just thanked God for me. This, cool, twenty-year-old, wanted to be like me, wow! I looked at her, hugged her, and then without another word she took my hand and led me out of the room into my Aunt's bay.

. . .

There's so much I wanted to say and ask but seeing Aunt Eliza laying on the bed totally shifted my focus. Even though the nurse had told Dad she was OK, seeing her lying there, eyes closed and very still, made me feel sick.

I walked over slowly, almost not wanting to approach. Were they sure she was okay? She didn't look it to me. That's when it hit me. I'd never seen Aunt Eliza asleep before. I always went to bed before her and by the time I woke up in the morning she was already busying herself in the kitchen. Seeing her now, felt weird, and different, and I really didn't like it.

I froze for a second just so my eyes could track her chest moving up and down. Phew, she was breathing.

I felt my nurse approaching behind me, then I heard, "Are you OK Sam?" Am I okay? I'm not sure. My tummy's not feeling great and suddenly I'm remembering how sore I'm feeling all over.

"May I please use the bathroom?" Were the words that flew out of my mouth this time around.

My nurse escorted me to a large white door with a huge silver handle, then pointed at it. "The toilet's in there Hun. Take your time and I'll be right out here waiting for you". "Thank you," I said before I ran in, locked the door, then took a moment to look at my face in the wall mirror situated just above the sink.

Oh boy was I going to be bruised. Already I could see a very dark patch around my left eye, the part of my face that hurt the most. Usually, I'd be worried about how these new additions to my face would affect how I'd look on my birthday but, if I'm honest, I was relieved. Relieved there was no blood, relieved that everything seemed to still be intact.

Remembering my nurse was outside and not wanting her to think I was going to the toilet-toilet, (if you know what I mean), I quickly freshened up and went back out.

This time as I approached the bay, Aunt Eliza's eyes were OPEN! My whole body was overcome with relief. I ran over to my precious godmother and gave her a big hug. I saw her wince a little and realised that I must have been hurting her. "I'm so sorry Aunty," I said as I quickly jumped off her. "It's fine sweetheart, it's so good to see you".

I stared at her, with my heart full of gladness to see that she was OK. I knew I had a mission to pray, but with that thought I remembered my nurse. As I turned to look for her, she was walking out of the ward. I opened my mouth to call her, then remembered I hadn't asked her name. In the distance, she turned, smiled, winked and just like that, she was gone.

I turned back to Aunt Eliza and a surge of energy entered my body. "Aunt Eliza, I need to pray for you!" And with that, I gently held her hand and began to pray.

CHAPTER 19

SAMANTHA'S DREAM

I've got some important news to share with everybody. If nobody has ever told you this before, then it's something you need to know. When you want time to fly, never sit in front of a clock and watch it. Doing that my friends, is a form of torture.

There was a large white clock on the wall next to Aunt Eliza's bay on the ward. The first time I looked at it, I genuinely wanted to know what time it was, but every time after that was just self-inflicted punishment.

I had no idea when Mum and Dad would arrive. I told myself they'd walk in the room at the top of the hour; at five o'clock, six o'clock, and seven o'clock. Every minute felt like it took an hour to pass.

. . .

I ate a sandwich, got treated to lots of mini packs of biscuits and even watched a film on my phone with Aunt Eliza. Well, I watched a film, while Aunt Eliza lay listening with her eyes closed commenting every now and then until the comments just sounded muffled and I realised she was falling asleep.

I've never understood how people can sleep in the middle of the day. That was until today. I yawned so much, that, at one point it felt like my mouth was open more than it was closed. I was so tired that I actually managed to make myself comfortable in the padded burgundy faux leather chair that was next to Aunt Eliza's bed.

I told myself, I'd just rest my eyes for a little while. I wouldn't fall asleep; I mean I never sleep during the day...

* * *

Samantha's dream

I hadn't been to this place before. The hustle and bustle of the crowd was almost daunting but with each step I made the crowd cleared a path for me to walk. Each step I took brought me closer and closer to a huge circular stage, in the middle of a large open field.

. . .

The closer I got, the more clearly I could see the back of a person on the stage. It was a woman. She was ministering a silent message to the crowd and they were engrossed. I couldn't hear a word she was saying but I knew, whatever it was, it must have been powerful.

She was almost glowing when I looked at her pacing up and down the stage. Even though I couldn't hear a word that she was saying, I could hear comments from people in the crowd. I heard someone say, "Just look at the anointing on her, it's amazing". I figured that's what the glow was, her anointing. Wow, she was a sight to behold.

The closer I got to the stage the more familiar this lady started to feel to me. I recognised her figure, I recognised her hair, I recognised the feeling I felt inside as I walked closer and closer, it was Aunt Eliza, wow!

With every step I took the excitement built stronger and stronger inside. It didn't take long before I was power walking, then jogging slightly, then running, all the way to the foot of the stage. The faster I moved, the faster the crowd parted. I just wanted to get to her.

. . .

I was only a few steps away and clearly, I couldn't wait, I shouted, "Aunt Eliza, it's me Sam!"

The figure on the stage stopped preaching the silent message, turned her head slowly and took two slow and measured steps to turn and look at me. I gasped and stopped in my tracks...

The woman on the stage wasn't Aunt Eliza at all...
IT WAS ME!

I stood there in amazement, staring up at myself, then through sheer shock and a bit of fear, I jumped up out of my sleep. My heart racing and desperately trying to catch my breath.

I must have startled Aunt Eliza because she woke up too calling me, "Samantha Pumpkin, are you alright?"

CHAPTER 20

WOMEN SHOULD BE SEEN AND NOT HEARD

My head thought... Dreams have meanings and Aunt Eliza is so wise. Maybe she could tell me what my dream means but my mouth said... "I'm alright Aunty, sorry for waking you".

"That's okay sweetheart. As long as you're good". Aunt Eliza responded as she shut her eyes and rested her head back down on her pillow.

My heart was still racing. It was just a dream, it wasn't real, but it had really affected me. What could it have meant?

As soon as the thought popped up in my head, I heard Aunt Eliza say clearly, "Don't search too hard for the meaning, take it for what it is".

. . .

Huh? What did she? How did she? What was going on?

"I didn't say anything Aunty," I said with a weird intonation that made it sound more like a question than a statement.

Eyes still closed, Aunt Eliza replied, "I know you didn't, but I did.".

"But how did you know?" I said, puzzled and amazed.

"I didn't. God just told me to say that to you, I figured you could explain why?"

Now when people tell me they hear God speaking to them, it fills me with so many questions. Did you really hear His voice? What does He sound like? Explain it to me and don't leave out any details, because I need to understand.

But this time, I couldn't think of one question to ask, all I could say, without sounding too much like Martin Luther King Jr, was; "I had a dream".

I described the sights and sounds of my dream with such detail, that I'm sure Aunt Eliza could have smelt the freshly cut grass on that field. But before I could stop and ask Aunt Eliza what she thought it meant, I started pouring out six weeks' worth of impressions, words from God and all the other signs I had been receiving.

With each new part of the story Aunt Eliza's smile grew bigger and bigger. I told her about the words from the youth pastors, the poster in my room, the garden, the definitions, I told her everything!

At the end of my summary of six-weeks-in-ten-minutes, I ended by saying, "It just feels like this has all happened for a reason, but I can't think of what that reason is!!"

At that point Aunt Eliza changed my life forever.

She shuffled herself up slightly in her bed, opened her eyes and looked in my direction. (For the first time in six weeks I realised that Aunt Eliza wasn't just looking beyond me because she was multitasking and looking at something else as she spoke to me. Her eyesight was really bad.)

She smiled the biggest smile I had ever seen and she said, "Sam baby-girl. God is calling you to Minister to the nations as He did to me on my 11th birthday. The anointing on your life is already so strong. That's why the twins aren't nice to you.

Sam, it's not you they don't like, but the badness in them gets angry with the goodness in you".

"I had the same thing when growing up with the young people I was surrounded by. The only difference was, back then, I received my call from God, but the people around me didn't believe me. It wasn't the done thing to allow women to preach, let alone an eleven-year-old little girl. As women, we made up the majority of the church, but were expected to be seen and not heard".

"My pastors, the church elders and even my parents discouraged me whenever I would plead with them to let me share a word I had received from God. For years I battled with the urgency of fulfilling my God given purpose matched with the disapproval of the people around me".

"By my late teens I grew tired and by the age of 21 something in me gave up. During a Sunday Service, the Lord gave me a word for one of the Deacons. I was so scared to say it, but the Lord opened my mouth and it just came out. I wanted to run but God would have me stay right where I was. Now the message (while not my message) was met with great disapproval. I was disciplined publicly and something inside me died a little. I never gave up on the Lord Sam, but I grew tired of fighting. I sat for years in churches propping up the pews, knowing I should be doing so much more. It's only in the past few years that I've become more of an active member of the church and have become determined once again to fulfil my God-given purpose here on Earth".

***"Sam, God is calling you to be a Prophet to the nations.* Answer your call, walk in it with confidence and never let anybody steer you off course Pumpkin. You've got this because God's got you".**

And with that Aunt Eliza closed her eyes, placed her head back on her pillow, and appeared to fall right back into a deep sleep.

"Whoa!"

CHAPTER 21

THE CALL

Dear Diary,

It's my birthday today. Eleven at long last. I start my new school in three days, and I am really excited about it. My face is looking really bruised but Dad keeps calling them my war wounds, which I think sounds quite cool. He says it'll be a great conversation starter when trying to speak to new people, so I'm slowly getting used to the idea of being, 'the girl with the bruised face' for a few weeks.

But that's not what I've sat down to write today. My news is so much more exciting than that...

GOD HAS CALLED ME!

. . .

And when I say called, I mean CALLED. I was fast asleep last night when I heard, ***"Samantha"*** I jumped up and ran into the spare room and said, "Yes Aunt Eliza, are you OK?"

Aunt Eliza is staying with us for a little while, just until she gets herself back on her feet. Having Aunt Eliza here with me in my house is a dream come true. But let me get back to the story.

I rushed in so fast I hadn't realised that Aunt Eliza was still fast asleep. I'd made her jump out of her sleep. "I didn't call you Pumpkin," she uttered softly, so I apologised and turned, ready to go back to my room.

I knew I heard my name, and the voice sounded like Aunt Eliza's. I began to wonder if like her eyesight, her memory was starting to go.

It suddenly dawned on me that the twins may have been playing a not-so-funny joke on me. I tipped toe back to the room and looked down at the inflatable bed to see them both fast asleep. So much so I could see Harry's big toe touching Patricia's face. Now there is no way she would have let that happen, even if she did want to play a trick on me.

. . .

I was so confused. I jumped back into bed, but it felt like my tiredness had left me. I sat up, put my night light on and opened my Bible to 1 Samuel chapter 1 (or first Sam as I now call it).

I read about a lady named Hannah, who was unable to have a baby. She prayed and God blessed her with one. It reminded me so much of the story my Mum had shared with me when I was at the hospital and reminded me of how Awesome God is.

I was still, clearly tired because as I got to the end of the chapter my eyes started stinging. I laid down again and drifted back to sleep. That's when I heard the voice again, ***"Samantha"***. I don't even remember jumping out of bed this time. I just know I was standing at the door of the spare room and everybody was fast asleep. This time I whispered not wanting to startle Aunt Eliza, "Yes Aunty, I'm here".

Unlike before Aunt Eliza opened her eyes and looked in my direction. "Samantha sweetie, the next time you hear the voice call you say: "Here I am Lord, I'm listening".

My heart was racing. What was Aunt Eliza saying? "Hold-up, what?" I whispered into the room, edging my way in ever so slightly so that Aunt Eliza would know that I was ready to talk. She just rolled on her side with her back facing me and said, "Good night Samantha".

. . .

That was an 'end of discussion' manoeuvre, so I knew I couldn't push my luck. I went back to bed, very nervous and not wanting to sleep again at all. I thought about picking up my Bible, but I didn't want to read, I couldn't read, I was too busy trying to figure out in my mind exactly what it was Aunt Eliza was saying to me.

I felt a little vulnerable, so I jumped under my duvet, covered my head and started humming to myself.

At what point I fell asleep; I do not know. All I do know is I heard the voice again. It felt louder and so much clearer this time... ***"Samantha".***

I sat up in bed and said exactly what Aunt Eliza had told me to say: "Here I am Lord, I'm listening".

Now what happened next could fill a whole new diary, but it's morning now and I really want to go and open my birthday presents. What I will say though is this… God spoke to me!

He confirmed my call as a Prophet(ess) to nations; gave me some important messages to deliver and then surrounded me with His Love.

. . .

Plain old simple Sam, an 11-year-old girl from Milton Keynes. If God can use me, He can use anybody.

Look out for the signs and be ready to answer your call. Until next time diary, this is Samantha the Prophetess signing out.

NOTES

ABOUT THE AUTHORS

IYWANA WRIGHT

Extra Printable Worksheets from: www.IywanaWright.com

Iywana Wright *is the pen name for Kimberley, Jeanette and Camelle:*

Kimberley Lawson is a Teacher, Photographer and Freelance Writer.

Jeanette McCarthy is a Freelance Writer, Researcher, Poet and Podcaster. This is her second published work.

Camelle Daley is an Entrepreneur, Business Coach & Speaker. This is her second published work

Our desire is to inspire the next generation in their walk with God, hearing His voice and walking in their purpose.

ALSO BY THE AUTHORS

God, Me, & Poetry by Jeanette McCarthy

www.JeanetteMcCarthy.com

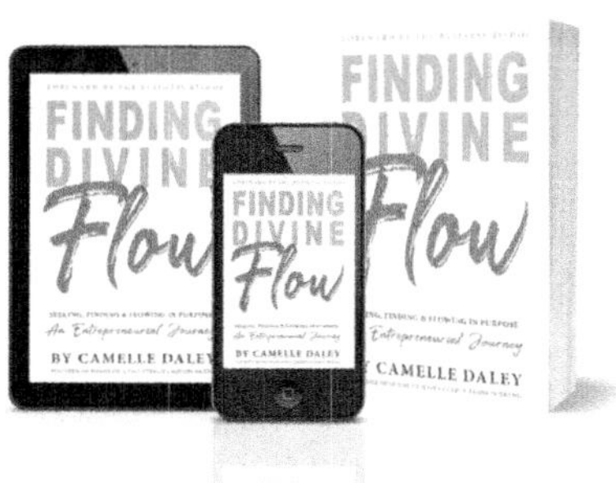

Finding Divine Flow by Camelle Daley

www.FindingDivineFlow.com

GLOSSARY

glitter

glitter /ˈɡlɪtə /

▸ verb [no object] **shine with a bright, shimmering reflected light**:

the grass glittered with dew.

▪ (of eyes) shine with a particular emotion:

her eyes glittered with excitement.

▸ noun

1 [in singular] **a bright, shimmering reflected light**:

the blue glitter of the sea.

▪ an expression of an emotion in a person's eyes:

the scathing glitter in his eyes.

2 [mass noun] **tiny pieces of sparkling material used for decoration**:

sneakers trimmed with sequins and glitter.

3 [mass noun] **an attractive and exciting but superficial quality**:

he avoids the glitter of show business.

– PHRASES

all that glitters is not gold proverb

the attractive external appearance of something is not a reliable indication of its true nature.

– ORIGIN late Middle English : from Old Norse glitra.

Oxford Dictionary

* * *

The Composition of Glitter:

Commercial **glitter** ranges in size from 0.002 to .25 inches (0.05 to 6.35 mm) a side. First, flat multi-layered sheets are produced combining plastic, colouring, and reflective material such as aluminium, titanium dioxide, iron oxide, and bismuth oxychloride.

www.wikipedia.org/wiki/Glitter

* * *

Anointing is Chron; it is confined to sacred and symbolic anointings; of Christ as the "Anointed" of God. It is used in connection with Kings, priests, and, prophets.

Anointing is Enchrio - Primarly, to rub in, to anoint.

Vines Complete Expository
Dictionary of Old & New Testament Words

Anointing is the ritual act of pouring aromatic oil over a person's head or entire body. By extension, the term is also applied to related acts of sprinkling, dousing, or smearing a person or object with any perfumed oil, milk, butter, or other fat.

Wikipedia

DISCUSSION QUESTIONS

USE THESE QUESTIONS FOR INDIVIDUAL REFLECTION OR FOR DISCUSSION WITH FRIENDS OR IN A SMALL GROUP. THEY WILL HELP YOU TO UNDERSTAND SAM'S JOURNEY AND HELP INTEGRATE THE MESSAGE OF THE STORY INTO YOUR OWN LIFE.

QUESTION 1

CHAPTER 2

In Chapter Two 'Saying goodbye to Mum and Dad'. We see Sam is apprehensive about her parents going away and spending her six weeks summer holiday with her godmother. Sam says a prayer to remind her of the bigger mission.

Write down or discuss when you have had to remind yourself of something more important than how you were feeling?

QUESTION 2

CHAPTER 2

To help her feel calm and remind her of what is most important, Sam decides to pray. Have you ever prayed to God when you were feeling uncertain about something?

Write down or discuss what you prayed about. If you've never prayed before why not write in the space below a short prayer about whatever is on your mind. Like Sam, ask God to be with you and trust that He will be.

CHAPTER 3

At the end of Chapter Three when Sam is missing her parents, she remembers how her Dad told her to pray whether she feels worried, lonely, afraid, happy or excited. She quotes a bible verse that says; 'Pray without ceasing,' which reminds her that it's better to pray than to worry all day.

God is interested in every part of your life, big or small. Did you know you can talk to God about everything, good and bad?

QUESTION 4

CHAPTER 7

In Chapter Seven, Sam shares with Harry that she learned about some of the ways God speaks, from the Youth Pastor, while attending her church group. Do you think God has ever spoken to you?

Write down how God has spoken to you.

(Remember it should ALWAYS match the ways God speaks in the Bible.)

QUESTION 5

CHAPTER 11

In Chapter Eleven, Sam is concerned about Harry and Patricia's behaviour. Her Dad reminds her during a phone call that she is a leader not a follower.

Are you a leader or a follower?

Do you find it easy to choose to do the right thing even if you may have to stand alone?

Write down your thoughts below and ask God to help develop your character to do the right thing even if no one else does.

QUESTION 6

CHAPTER 18

In Chapter Eighteen, Sam shows kindness and courage when she prays for the nurse. Sam took time to encourage her, even though she has just been through an upsetting experience with her Aunt.

Ask God to help you; see the needs of others around you, to give you the wisdom to know how to help, give you the courage to help and to do it with kindness.

How easy do you find it to pray for others?

QUESTION 7

CHAPTER 21

In Chapter Twenty-One, Sam knows her purpose. That God has called her to be a Prophet. Everyone has at least one natural gift or talent. But God also gives us spiritual gifts. And God has given everyone a purpose in life. We can all make a difference and touch the lives of others.

Write down what you enjoy, then ask God which one of those things you could use to help someone else. Maybe you're good at math and your friend isn't so you could tutor them. Maybe you like baking and you could make cookies for your local care home. Or sell them and give the money to charity.

Do you know what you are good at? What do you love to do?

Spiritual gifts are received when you become a Christian and are given to help others and to be used in a loving way.

Ask God which one(s) He has given you.

To learn more, you can read these passages in the Bible.

1 Corinthians chapters 12,13 and 14

Romans chapter 12 verses 4 - 8

Ephesians chapter 4 verses 7 -12

THE VOICE OF GOD

When God speaks it is ALWAYS for our good and never to harm us or anyone else.

The best way to get to know someone is to spend time with them. God has given us the Bible so we can learn more about Him. Get to know God's character/nature by reading the Bible. So, when God speaks you can be sure what His voice sounds like.

If you want to learn more about God, start with reading the Gospel of St John to learn more about Jesus Christ.

* * *

What is a Prophet?

A Christian chosen by God to hear His voice and proclaim and teach the will of God to others. They are God's lawyers and voice on the earth. They are called to confront and bring order. They root out, pull down, destroy, throw down, build and plant, both in the natural and spiritual realm. Jeremiah 1:5-9

What is the gift of Prophecy?

A Christian who has learned to follow the leading of God's Spirit (often called the Holy Spirit) and who speaks the mind and will of God to edify, comfort and encourage others. 1 Corinthians 14:1

What is the Spirit of Prophecy?

Any Christian in a prophetic atmosphere can be used by God to share a word that proclaims who Jesus is. This does not mean the person has the gift of prophecy and definitely does not mean they are a Prophet. Revelation 19:10

BECOMING A CHRISTIAN

What does the Bible say?

Romans 10: 8-13

(8) But what does it say? "The word is near you, in your mouth and in your heart" (that is, the word of faith which we preach):

(9) that if you confess with your mouth the Lord Jesus and believe in your heart that God has raised Him from the dead, you will be saved.

(10) For with the heart one believes unto righteousness, and with the mouth confession is made unto salvation.

(11) For the Scripture says, "Whoever believes on Him will not be put to shame."

(12) For there is no distinction between Jew and Greek, for the same Lord over all is rich to all who call upon Him.

(13) For "whoever calls on the name of the LORD shall be saved."

Think About It:

God created us to know and live in His love. He created us for a purpose and to have meaning in our lives. He died on the cross for our sins, so we could find hope and true life in Christ.

All you have to do is ask Jesus, with a sincere heart, to forgive you for all the wrong things you have done, and ask Him to give you His free gift of Salvation and to come into your heart as your Lord and Saviour. Then thank Him for answering your prayer.

God loves you and there is nothing you can ever do to change that truth. If you are ready to make that decision. Pray this prayer from your heart to Jesus.

SALVATION PRAYER

Dear Lord Jesus,

I acknowledge my sinful ways and that you died on the cross for me. I have lived my life without you, and I want that to change today. I ask you to forgive me, wash away my sins and cleanse me.

I believe in my heart and confess with my mouth Jesus Christ is Lord and rose from the dead. I surrender my life to you and ask you Jesus to be my Lord and Saviour. I turn from my selfish ways and receive your gift of salvation. Give me a new heart, fill me with your Holy Spirit and empower me to live by faith in you every day.

Thank you for making me brand new. I trust you with my life.

In Jesus' Name,

Amen.

PROPHETS IN THE BIBLE

SOME OF THE PROPHETS IN THE BIBLE YOU COULD STUDY

Jesus
Miriam
Deborah
Anna
Huldah
Samuel
Joseph
Daniel
Ezekiel
Isaiah
Hosea
Jonah
Zechariah
Malachi
Nathan
Habakkuk
John the Baptist

A CHARITY CLOSE TO OUR HEARTS

Esther Children's Home, Ghana

A place where the orphans, motherless and fatherless children are raised to become shinning stars in the society.

www.EstherChildrensHome.com

Printed in Great Britain
by Amazon

44984557R00088